Join the Cutiecorns on every adventure!

Heart of Gold

Purrfect Pranksters

Purrfect Pranksters

by Shannon Penney
illustrated by Addy Rivera Sonda

SCHOLASTIC INC.

Text copyright © 2020 by Shannon Decker
Illustrations copyright © 2020 by Addy Rivera Sonda

All rights reserved. Published by Scholastic Inc., *Publishers since
1920*. SCHOLASTIC and associated logos are trademarks and/or
registered trademarks of Scholastic Inc.

The publisher does not have any control over and does not assume any
responsibility for author or third-party websites or their content.

ISBN 978-1-338-54038-3
10 9 8 7 6 5 4 3 2 1   20 21 22 23 24

Printed in the U.S.A. 40
First printing 2020

Book design by Jennifer Rinaldi

Scholastic Inc., 557 Broadway, New York, NY 10012
Scholastic UK Ltd., Euston House, 24 Eversholt Street, London NW1 1DB
Made in Jefferson City, USA

Chapter 1

"Do it again, Flash!" Glitter giggled, clapping her paws.

Flash concentrated really hard. She focused all her energy on a dandelion growing along the side of the road. Her purple horn gleamed. The dandelion suddenly rose into the air, almost as if it were plucked from the ground by an invisible paw. It zoomed over to Glitter and tucked itself behind her fluffy white ear.

"That was puptastic!" Glitter barked. "Bow wow, you're getting really good at using your shifting magic already, Flash."

Flash grinned proudly, holding her snout high. "Thanks! It's so much fun finally learning to use our powers, isn't it?"

The two pups lived on Puppypaw Island, a pawsome place filled with rolling meadows, winding dirt lanes, and golden beaches. Barking Bay, the town at the center of it all, was bright, bustling, and brimming with magic. That's because the pups who lived there weren't ordinary dogs at all. They were Cutiecorns! Each pup had a colorful unicorn horn on his or her head—and magical powers to go along with it.

"Thanks for waiting," came a voice from

behind them. Twinkle, their blue-horned Beagle friend, joined Flash and Glitter at the end of the lane.

"Twinkle!" Flash yipped, running circles around her pal. "Want me to use my magic to pick a dandelion for you?"

Twinkle rolled her eyes, smiling. "I would love that, but I think we need to get going. We shouldn't be late for school!"

The three friends trotted along toward school, barking up a storm as they went. They paused at a little brick house along the way to pick up Sparkle, a Golden Retriever with a shimmering horn to match her fur.

"What do you think we're going to learn today?" she asked, falling into step next to Flash.

"I don't know!" Flash said, giving a little

leap of excitement. "But whatever it is, I'm sure it will be ter-ruff-ic!"

So far, Cutiecorn Academy was even more pawfect than Flash had dreamed it would be. The teachers and other pups were furbulous, and Flash had never imagined all the different kinds of magic they'd get to learn. It was a pup's paradise!

As the pups crested Howl Hill, they could suddenly see all of Barking Bay spread out below. Off to one side, the water stretched all the way to the horizon. Small boats were docked in the cove at the bottom of Howl Hill, and Flash could see her dad's familiar blue boat tied to the dock. Cutiecorn Academy sat nestled in the hillside, gleaming white among the green grass and blooming flowers.

"Race you!" Flash yapped, taking off before her friends could even bark. She heard them laugh as their paws thundered along behind her. She may have been small, but Flash was fast!

Suddenly, she felt herself tumble snout over paws. She turned somersaults, finally rolling to a stop.

"Flash, are you okay?" Glitter appeared at her side, a look of concern on her snout. Sparkle and Twinkle were right behind her.

Flash grinned. "I'm fine—I must have just stumbled over my own four paws!"

Sparkle stepped forward. "No, you didn't." She held up the end of a long daisy chain, woven together with little white flowers, grass, and . . .

"Is that . . . seaweed?" Flash asked, poking the chain with her paw.

"It sure is," Sparkle said with a nod. "Strange! This chain was stretched across the hillside path."

Twinkle took a closer look. "It seems like someone was trying to trip up pups."

"What about the seaweed? Whoever made this chain must have come from down by the water," Glitter noted thoughtfully.

Flash got to her paws and wrapped the daisy chain into a neat loop. "Well, they got me, but let's make sure no other pups become falling fur balls." She set the chain off to one side of the path. "Before my ter-ruff-ic tumble, I believe we were racing!"

Without another word, Flash took off as fast as her paws would carry her. She raced under the school archway with Glitter, Sparkle, and Twinkle right on her tail. They all tumbled into a heap on the grass in front of the building, panting and howling with laughter. They had barely caught their breath when a chime rang out. They had arrived just in time—school was starting! The four friends got to their paws and headed through the open doors to their classroom.

"Good morning, Cutiecorns!" Mrs. Horne, the head of Cutiecorn Academy, stood at the front of the room. She clapped her paws for attention and grinned around at the pups. "I hope you're all rested up and ready for your first magic lesson of the day, Feeling Your Magic!"

Flash glanced over at Sparkle and winked. Sparkle was especially good at feeling magic. Every pup had different strengths, but it was important that they learn and practice all kinds of magical skills. Who knew when they would come in handy?

"Now, a key part of feeling your magic is being able to feel it in all different situations," Mrs. Horne explained. "Some pups can access their magic more easily when they're scared, for example. Some can do it best when they're relaxed, or surprised, or even sad. It's my job to teach you to find it anytime, anywhere!"

Flash thought about the first time she had really used her magic. She and her friends had faced off against a sinister cat named Claw, and Flash had been able to use her shifting magic to trap the cat so they could escape. She had been scared out of her fur!

Mrs. Horne split the pups into small

groups and had them practice finding their magic in different situations. One corner of the room was set up like a birthday party, with music, dancing, and snacks. Another was draped with fabric to make it dark and shadowy, with a chilly breeze and spooky sounds. A different area had cozy dog beds and a movie playing quietly on a small TV. As the pups settled into the different areas, it was easy to forget they were in class! Mrs. Horne visited each group and worked with them on locating their magic. Bow wow, what fun!

It seemed like no time had passed when the chime rang out again. All twelve pups in the class groaned.

Mrs. Horne laughed merrily. "I'm glad you all enjoyed today's lesson so much! We'll do more next time, pup's honor. See you then!"

As she walked back into the hall with her friends, Flash couldn't help jumping up and doing a little flip. The day was off to a pawfect start!

Chapter 2

Flash was sure her day could only get better. After all, their next lesson was Shifting Magic—her specialty!

"What do you think we're going to move today?" Glitter asked, pushing open the classroom door.

Flash thought for a minute. "I don't know. Maybe more dandelions, or—"

"Butterflies!" Twinkle interrupted.

"Ooh, butterflies would be fun!" Flash said. "I hope you're right, Twinkle."

Twinkle pointed a paw into the classroom. "I wasn't guessing. Look!"

As Flash stepped into the room, she could hardly believe her eyes. It was filled with a swarm of colorful butterflies! They fluttered about wildly, blurs of color zooming from one side of the room to the other. Grrrrreat!

"What's going on?" Sparkle barked as the rest of their classmates joined them in the doorway. Everyone jostled to get a better look at the butterflies.

"Do you think it's a test?" Flash asked excitedly. "Maybe we have to use our magic to capture all these butterflies!"

"If that's the case, our lesson is heading out the window," Twinkle said.

Glitter gasped. "Oh no!"

Sure enough, the swarm of butterflies had found an open classroom window. Now they were looping and swooping out into the fresh air. Before the pups could even bark, every butterfly had darted through the window and out of sight.

"Well, that was strange," Sparkle said, walking into the now-empty classroom with her friends.

Flash dashed over to the open window. "Come back, butterflies!" she barked out into the sunny courtyard. "We promise we won't transform your wings into bat wings or anything—we're not that good at magic yet!"

Flash's classmates all laughed, joining her at the window to see if they could glimpse any of the escaped butterflies. They were already gone, but Flash thought she could hear soft giggles coming from somewhere outside the window. Strange!

"Hello, pups!" a voice called out. The pups

spun around to see their teacher, Mr. Magictail, standing behind them. He was a big Chocolate Lab with a fiery red horn and a wide, friendly grin. "What's so interesting out there?"

Twinkle calmly explained, "When we got here, the room was filled with butterflies—"

"But they escaped out the window and now they're gone! Ruff luck, right?" Flash didn't mean to interrupt her friend, but she just couldn't stop herself from barking up.

Mr. Magictail frowned, then trotted to the front of the room. A few large cages with mesh sides sat on his desk. The doors on all the cages were wide open. Woof!

"I had planned to use those butterflies for our lesson today," he explained to the class. "You all did such a ter-ruff-ic job shifting immobile objects last week, I thought we'd try shifting something that moves on its own—and not necessarily where you want it to go."

Flash couldn't help bouncing on her paws a little. Flying fur balls, that sounded like fun!

"What will we do now that the butterflies are gone?" asked Fuzz, a Collie with a green horn the color of fresh-cut grass.

Mr. Magictail thought for a minute, then clapped his paws. "I guess we'll just have to try something different." He pulled a box of beads and string out of his desk. "Each of you can take a pawful of beads and a piece of string. Try using your magic to thread the beads onto the string." He winked. "This is tricky, so don't get discouraged if you can't master it today. You can always just work on moving the beads from one spot to another."

The pups all barked excitedly as they collected their beads and string and moved to different areas of the room to practice.

Flash dumped her beads into a pile and immediately began moving them through the air with her magic. She could feel her purple horn gleaming as the magic flowed through

every piece of her fur. She concentrated hard on threading a bead onto her string. It took a few tries, but soon she got it—hot dog!

Flash glanced over at Twinkle, who was using her magic to arrange beads in an orderly row by size and shape. She hadn't put any on her string yet, but Flash was impressed with her friend's skills. Just last week, Twinkle had trouble shifting anything at all!

"Pawsome job, Twinkle," she whispered with a grin.

Twinkle smiled back. "Thanks! It's hard work, but I think I'm getting the hang of it."

Flash sighed. "I hope we get to shift butterflies sometime soon. That sounded like a ter-ruff-ic lesson!"

"Yeah, until someone ruined it by letting

the butterflies out," Twinkle said gruffly. "Barking bulldogs, who would have done something like that?"

Flash thought about it, scratching her snout. Everyone at Cutiecorn Academy was there for the same reason—to learn to use magic. Who would have purposely spoiled their lesson? And why?

"Bow wow!" Flash said, suddenly wiggling with excitement. "Between this and the daisy chain this morning, we have a bone-ified mystery on our paws!"

Chapter 3

The pups couldn't stop barking about the great butterfly escape for the rest of the school day. The afternoon passed in a blur of chatter, laughter, and amazing magic lessons. There was so much to learn!

As Flash and her friends headed out through the school gates, the sun was warm on their fur. Flash sighed happily.

"It's a beautiful day, isn't it?" Glitter said, trotting alongside her friend. "The pawfect day for a milkshake." She winked.

Flash giggled. She had just been thinking that! Glitter was especially good at caring magic, so she could often tell what her puppy pals were thinking and feeling.

"I have to visit the outdoor market anyway," Flash said. "I told my mom I'd pick up a jar of peanut butter on the way home. My dad got home late last night, and he was so hungry from his trip that he had three peanut butter sandwiches!" Flash's dad was an explorer, and he often sailed to far-flung islands to learn about other Cutiecorns and their customs. "Want to come, pups?"

"Fur real, of course we do!" Sparkle said.

"Now what's this I heard about milkshakes?"

Together, the four friends hurried down the rolling hillside into Barking Bay. The outdoor market was right in the center of town, and it was always filled with bright colors, fun music, and lots of Cutiecorns! Today was no different. As the pups set paw in the market, they hardly knew where to look first. There were booths with colorful striped awnings in every direction, selling food, toys, crafts, and anything else Flash and her friends could dream of.

"First stop, milkshakes!" Glitter declared, heading for the Cutiecorn Confections booth. She turned to look at her friends over her shoulder. "My treat—I have some allowance that I've been saving for a sweet treat!"

Before long, Flash, Glitter, Sparkle, and Twinkle were wandering from booth to booth, sipping their milkshakes happily. Flash bought a big jar of peanut butter, just like her mom had asked. As she heaved the bag up onto her shoulder, she groaned. "Doggone, this is heavier than a box of bones! How am I ever going to make it home?"

"Don't worry," Twinkle said with a lop-sided grin. "We can take turns carrying it."

They paused to watch a juggler in front of the fountain in Sniff and Ruff Square. Flash set the bag down next to her, rubbing her shoulder with one paw. She made a mental note to add juggling to the list of skills she wanted to learn. Maybe she could use her magic to move the balls through the air—paws-free

juggling! Wouldn't that be puptastic?

"Ooh, can we try on some silly hats?" Sparkle asked, pointing a paw at a nearby booth. The other pups agreed (even though Twinkle rolled her eyes a little).

But as her friends began walking toward the hat booth, Flash yelped in surprise. "Wait up, pups! My bag—it's gone!"

Sure enough, the bag wasn't next to Flash,

where she had set it down only minutes before. "It was right here! How could it have disappeared from under my snout?"

Twinkle, Sparkle, and Glitter started sniffing around the market as Flash retraced her pawsteps. She remembered setting the bag down at the fountain, and she hadn't moved a paw since then!

A moment later, Twinkle barked, "I found it!" As the other pups rushed to her side, she pulled Flash's bag out from behind a yellow bench.

"But how did it get there?" Sparkle wondered aloud. "We never even walked by this bench."

Twinkle frowned. "You're right! This doesn't make any sense."

Flash bounced on her paws. "Thanks for

tracking it down, Twinkle. Now, let's not waste any more time—we have to get over to those silly hats!"

The four friends raced to the hat booth, and soon they were howling with laughter. Glitter, wearing a motorcycle helmet with flames on the sides, plopped a frilly pink hat on Twinkle's head. "Oh, it's pawfect!" she

cried, clapping her paws. Twinkle scowled, but even she had to laugh when she looked at her reflection in the mirror.

Sparkle tried a tall, pointed princess hat with a flowing tulle train. Flash grabbed a shiny red firefighter's helmet. "Who needs a Dalmatian when you could have Flash the Fire Pup?" she declared, giggling.

Around and around they went, dropping hats on one another's heads, until they'd tried every hat in the booth. As they hung the last few hats back on the rack, Glitter declared, "That was grrrreat!"

The others barked in agreement, heading out of the booth. It was almost time to go home for dinner.

"Wait!" Flash yipped. She looked around wildly. "My bag is gone again!"

"Again?" Sparkle asked, joining her.

Twinkle immediately put her snout to the ground. "Something fishy is going on here," she said, sniffing around the booth.

"You can say that again," Flash barked. "What does someone want with your peanut butter, anyway?"

"I don't think they want your peanut butter," Glitter said, trotting up. She had Flash's bag in her paw! "If they do, they're not doing a very good job of holding on to it."

Flash threw her paws around her friend. "Where did you find this?"

Glitter nodded toward the next booth over,

which sold fluffy pillows and cozy blankets. "It was sitting just inside that booth, tucked behind a pillow shaped like a dog bone."

"It seems like someone keeps hiding the bag from you, Flash," Sparkle said thoughtfully. "Almost like a prank."

"But who would do that?" Flash asked. "And why?"

Twinkle scratched her snout. "I don't know—but we're going to figure it out!"

Chapter 4

That night was Flash's favorite night of the week—movie night on the beach! All the Cutiecorns of Puppypaw Island gathered at dusk to munch on pupcorn and watch a movie under the stars. Bow wow, it was the best!

"Can we go now, Mom? Can we? Can we?"

Flash barked, racing in circles around her mom in their backyard.

"I'll tell you what," Flash's mom said. "You run on ahead. Dad and I will meet you at the movie in a little bit, when he wakes up from his nap. He's doggone tired out from his trip! Just bring a friend along with you. I'm sure Dash will be there soon, too." Flash's big brother was six years older, and he always kept an eye out for Flash and her friends.

"Really?" Flash yipped, clapping her paws. "Furbulous—thanks, Mom!" Without another word, she zipped around to the front yard and down the street.

Within minutes, Flash had gathered Sparkle, Twinkle, and Glitter from their houses. It was time to hit the beach!

"What movie do you think is playing tonight?" Sparkle asked as the four friends trotted down the winding path to the sand.

"Ooh, I hope it's that new one with Cruise McWoof," Twinkle said. "I've heard that it's action-packed!"

Flash sighed happily, setting paw on the warm, soft sand. "I don't even care what movie it is. I just love sitting with my bucket of pupcorn, watching a movie under the stars with my best friends."

Twinkle nudged her and smiled. "But I still hope it's the Cruise McWoof one," she said. All four pups giggled.

As they made their way down the beach, they could see that the outdoor movie theater up ahead was deserted.

"I guess we are pretty early," Flash said sheepishly.

Sparkle pointed a paw. "Why don't we go to the playground over there for a bit? We can run around until other pups start to show up."

"Ter-ruff-ic idea, Sparkle!" Glitter said. "I'll just put my blanket down near the movie screen to save our spot."

Barking happily, Flash, Glitter, Sparkle,

and Twinkle headed into the roped-off movie area—and stopped in their tracks.

"What happened here?" Twinkle said, frowning.

The large area in front of the movie screen was usually filled with soft sand, perfect for sitting or lying on. But today, large water-filled holes dotted the space! Towering sandcastles

decorated with rocks and shells stood between the holes, which meant there was hardly anywhere to sit. What a muttley mess!

Flash walked around carefully, surveying the scene. Flying fur balls! Who would have done something like this to their theater?

"It's a good thing we got here early," Glitter said. "Now we have time to clean this up before the movie starts!"

Flash couldn't help smiling at her friend. Glitter always managed to find the best in every situation.

Without another woof, the four friends got their tails in gear. It was pawsomely hard work, but soon the theater area was mostly back to normal, aside from some soggy sand.

Twinkle flopped down. "I'm one beat Beagle!" she said.

"Me too," Sparkle agreed, sitting next to her. "Well, except for the Beagle part," she said, laughing.

"Guess what, pups!" Flash barked. "The movie is starting!"

Twinkle, Sparkle, and Glitter jumped to their paws and settled into a spot in front of the screen. Flash circled them, giggling. "Hot diggity dog, Twinkle—look! It *is* the Cruise McWoof movie!"

Chapter 5

The next morning, Flash climbed out of bed and stretched her paws high over her head. Woof, she had really needed that sleep after such a crazy day! Luckily, it was Saturday, so she'd been able to sleep in. Paws down, that was the best thing about the weekend!

Flash grabbed her fuzzy robe, pulled it on, and shuffled out to the kitchen. Her dad was

cooking sizzling bacon on the stove, Dash was chowing down on a huge plate of food, and her mom was drinking from a mug of tea.

"Bow wow, that bacon smells delicious!" Flash cried, giving her dad a hug.

"Help yourself," her dad said with a smile. "Are you feeling better after a good long sleep?"

Flash piled some scrambled eggs and bacon on a plate. "Definitely!" she barked. "Yesterday was just such a strange day, it made me dog-tired."

"I don't understand who would have piled sand and water all over the outdoor movie theater," her mom said. "It was kind of you and your friends to clean it up, though. I'm proud of you!"

Flash blushed. "Thanks. But I didn't even get to tell you about the other weird things that happened!" She was feeling more awake now, and the eggs and bacon were giving her energy. She began talking, faster and faster.

"So first, I tripped over this daisy chain on the way to school. It was made out of flowers, but also seaweed. Weird, right? Then we walked into class and it was swarming with butterflies. They were fluttering all over the room like some sort of crazy, colorful tornado. Pup's honor! And after school, we went to the market, and my bag kept disappearing. I'd put it down for a minute, go to pick it up, and it would be gone! We always found it nearby, but in someplace I hadn't even set paw in. It was puptastically creepy!" She finally paused to take a breath and shovel some more food into her mouth.

Her dad looked thoughtful. He was used to listening to Flash bark on and on, so Flash wasn't worried that he'd missed any of the details.

"That is awfully strange," Flash's dad said after a minute.

"Do you think someone is playing pranks on you?" Dash asked.

Flash shrugged. "Maybe, but the butter-flies and the movie theater affected lots of pups, not just me. Whoever did those things could have gotten in a lot of trouble if they'd been caught!"

Flash's mom nodded slowly. "That's true. Do you think there's anyone who—"

But she didn't have a chance to finish her sentence before they heard someone barking at the door.

"Flash! Flash! Come quick! You won't believe it!"

Flash ran to the door and flung it open. Twinkle stood just outside, panting. Her eyes were wide.

Before Flash could even ask what was going on, Twinkle said, "You have to see what's happening in town. Come on!" She turned on her paws and raced back to the road.

Flash looked at her mom, her dad, and Dash. Then all four of them bolted after Twinkle, leaving their bathrobes behind. What in the world could she be barking about? What strange thing could have happened this time?

As the five of them ran down the dirt road into town, more and more pups seemed to be barking up a storm. Cutiecorns of all ages came out of their houses to see what the fuss was about. Soon, the different roads to Barking Bay were filled with curious pups!

As they rounded the corner into the square, she finally saw what everyone was barking about.

The large fountain in the center of the square was filled with bright purple water! But worse, it was also filled with bubbles, which poured out of the fountain and onto the street. Purple bubbles oozed everywhere!

Cutiecorns appeared from streets in every direction, barking in confusion at the sight. The bubbles began to fill the square, so no

pup could get close enough to the fountain to stop it. Bow wow!

"What a mess!" Flash said, taking in the scene.

"I know," Twinkle barked, nodding grimly. "Whoever is pulling these pranks has put a paw over the line with this one."

Chapter 6

"What's happening, pups?" a familiar voice rang out. Sparkle trotted up, with Glitter right on her tail.

"Who turned Sniff and Ruff Square into a giant bubble bath?" Glitter asked in disbelief.

Flash shrugged. "Your guess is as good as

mine," she said. "But someone is trying to cause tons of trouble!"

The pups watched as Flash's parents and some other adult Cutiecorns put their snouts together and came up with a plan. Before long, they were positioned all around the square, using their magic to stop the fountain and pop the bubbles.

"Wow," Flash breathed, peering around at the glowing horns of different colors. She'd never seen so much magic all at once before!

Sure enough, the purple fountain stopped flowing. With no new bubbles forming, the Cutiecorns were able to use their magic to clean up the bubbles that had filled the square. Soon, all that was left was a slimy purple film

over the cobblestones. That wasn't something magic could fix—the pups would have to put their paws to work and get scrubbing!

Mrs. Handysnout, who owned the hardware store on the square, brought out piles of buckets, brushes, and sponges. Flash and her friends picked up a bucket, filled it with water from a nearby hose, and grabbed four sponges. It was time to get their tails in gear! Around the square, pups of all ages were doing the same. This was one of the things the Cutiecorns loved about living on Puppypaw Island. They could always count on one another, no matter what.

"We'll have this place cleaned up in no time," Flash cheered, scrubbing away at some purple goo. "It'll be shinier than Sparkle's fur!"

Sparkle laughed. "You're barking up the wrong tree, Flash. My fur is awfully shiny!"

The four friends chatted as they worked, and soon they'd cleared one big patch of cobblestones and moved on to another. Suddenly, Flash felt a funny shiver run through her fur. That was strange! The sun was high in the sky, and the square was warm in the golden light.

Flash glanced around. Wait—what was

that? Something darted into the shadows behind the Pupcorn Parlor.

"You guys," Flash said quietly, pointing a paw. "I just saw something over there . . . and it didn't look like a pup."

Glitter's eyes grew wide. "What do you think it was, Flash?"

"Oh, this is like Claw all over again," Sparkle said, slapping a paw over her eyes.

Flash thought about how Claw had stolen Sparkle's precious locket, and how the pups had tracked her down to reclaim it.

"Do you think she could be back?" Twinkle asked, looking at Flash closely.

Flash shook her head. "No, this thing was smaller. But it didn't move like a pup." She suddenly dropped her sponge. "Let's follow it!"

Twinkle groaned. "This really IS like Claw all over again," she grumbled, but she put her sponge down and trotted behind Flash, Sparkle, and Glitter toward the Pupcorn Parlor.

As they got closer, Flash stopped and put a paw to her mouth. "Nice and slow now," she said quietly.

"I don't think I've ever heard Flash suggest moving slowly," Twinkle whispered with a wink.

Together, the four pups stuck close to the yellow walls of the building, sneaking down one side and peeking around the back.

"I don't see anything," Sparkle said, disappointed.

Flash and Twinkle hung their snouts. What ruff luck!

But Glitter smiled. "We don't need to see," she said. "We just need to follow our magic!"

Of course! Why hadn't Flash thought of that? She threw her paws around Glitter. "You're a genius! What a barking good idea!"

All four friends stood side by side, concentrating hard. After a moment, the alley behind the Pupcorn Parlor filled with a warm, colorful light. Their horns had all begun to glow!

Sparkle was best at feeling magic, and she suddenly clapped her paws. "This way!" she called, running ahead.

As Flash fell into pawstep behind her friend, something caught her eye. "Look! Purple drips!" Sure enough, the cobblestones were splattered with drips of the same purple goo that filled Sniff and Ruff Square.

Now that they had their magic and the purple drips to follow, Flash and her friends were unstoppable! They dashed through a series of back alleyways, using both their eyes and their magic to lead the way.

Suddenly, Sparkle skidded to a halt, throwing out a paw to stop her friends from going any farther. Flash's nose told her they were somewhere near the alley behind the Pawfect Slice pizza shop, but she'd never been back there before. Up ahead, the alley opened into a little courtyard between a bunch of different buildings.

Sparkle pointed a paw, her eyes wide open in surprise. There was something in the courtyard!

Together, the four pups tiptoed to the end

of the alley. As they poked their snouts around the corner, what they saw almost made Flash bark out loud:

Kittens!

Chapter 7

Flash couldn't believe her eyes. She looked at her friends in disbelief.

"Four fuzzy little kittens have been behind all this trouble?" she whispered. "That can't be!"

Glitter nodded. "Look at their paws."

As Flash looked more closely, she could see that the four kittens were all different colors, but they had one thing in common—their paws were purple!

"Caught purple-pawed," she muttered.

The pups watched as the kittens frolicked around the courtyard, jumping and tumbling. The orange one climbed up on a brick wall, then pounced on the unsuspecting black-and-white one down below. They rolled ears over paws, giggling and batting at one another. Flash recognized those giggles from the classroom! These kittens didn't seem to have a care in the world! How could they have made so much mischief?

"Uh, guys?" Twinkle whispered suddenly. "Did you notice something else about the kittens?"

Flash looked again, and gasped. "They

have horns!" she yelped. Sure enough, each kitten had a small, colorful horn between its ears. Flash clapped a paw over her mouth. These kittens were Cutiecorns?

"I knew there were other kinds of Cutiecorns outside of Puppypaw Island, but I never thought I'd see them in the fur!" Sparkle said, awestruck.

Flash nodded in agreement. They'd always been taught that any type of animal could be a Cutiecorn—kittens, rabbits, hedgehogs, even birds or dolphins! But Puppypaw Island was so remote, seeing other kinds of Cutiecorns there was rare. Flash's dad had told her pup-loads of stories about his travels, though. As an explorer, he had visited all sorts of distant places and met all different kinds of Cutiecorns. It sounded ter-ruff-ically exciting! Now a little of that excitement had appeared here, on Puppypaw Island—and Flash and her friends were the first to discover it!

"So these aren't ordinary kittens," Twinkle added, keeping her eyes glued to the fur balls in the courtyard.

Just then, the gray kitten crouched down,

as if to pounce. She wiggled . . . she paused . . . and then she took a flying leap all the way across the courtyard!

"Barking bulldogs!" Flash yipped. "That was some leap!"

"You're telling me," Glitter said quietly. Suddenly, her eyes grew wide. "Look at that one!"

The calico cat was walking lightly across the courtyard. Without warning, her paws lifted off the ground and she began floating through the air! She tumbled this way and that, laughing and mewing. She knocked into a flowerpot, and it crashed to the ground and shattered. She floated the other way, recklessly, until she bounced against the side of a building. "I'm flyinggggg!" she cried, turning a somersault in the air.

The pieces were beginning to click into place in Flash's mind. When she turned to look at her friends, she could see that they understood, too.

She pointed a paw at the mischievous kittens. "So these kittens are Cutiecorns, which means . . ."

"They have magical powers," Sparkle finished.

Twinkle frowned. "But they don't seem to know how to use them properly. Their magic is totally out of control."

"This is kitten chaos!" Flash yipped, bouncing on her paws. The kittens may have been out of control, but they were also puptastically exciting! What wacky thing would they do next?

Glitter drew her friends into a huddle. "We need to put our snouts together, pups. If someone doesn't stop these kittens, things could get really crazy!"

"Aww, can't we let them stay awhile? Maybe we can all be friends!" Flash barked.

"Their families are probably worried sick,"

Glitter said. "Plus, it could be dangerous for us and for them if they can't control their magic."

Flash glanced back into the courtyard, where the orange kitten was racing around in circles at super-speed. "I can't stopppppp!" she cried, giggling.

"Should we go find a grown-up?" Sparkle asked.

All four pups paused, thinking hard.

"Let's try solving this problem ourselves first," Flash suggested. "Now that we know what we're looking for, these kittens are easy to find. They leave a trail of destruction wherever they go!"

Her friends nodded. "We'll have to be

quick on our paws," Twinkle said. "We need a plan, and we need one fast."

Flash grinned. "Luckily, being fast is one of my specialties!" she said with a wink.

Chapter 8

Flash, Glitter, Twinkle, and Sparkle ducked into the nearby Cuté Café and piled around a table. The café was a favorite spot for pups of all ages, full of cozy cushions, stacks of books, and colorful framed maps. Stepping inside always felt like starting off on some far-flung adventure!

Glitter grabbed lemonade and blueberry

muffins for everyone. All the excitement of the morning had made them doggone hungry!

"I do my best thinking on a full stomach," Flash said around a mouthful of muffin.

"You do *everything* on a full stomach," Twinkle said with a laugh. It was true—Flash had a reputation for being a tiny pup with a dog-sized appetite!

"So we need to stop the kittens before they destroy Barking Bay with their magic," Sparkle recapped. "But how?"

Glitter said softly, "We should send them back to wherever they came from. They're just little kittens. I'll bet their parents are terribly worried about them!"

"I don't think they'll go without a fight," Twinkle barked. "They seem like they're having too much fun here!"

Flash clapped her paws. "That's why we have to set a trap!" she cried. Some pups at nearby tables looked over at them curiously. "Oops, sorry," Flash whispered, lowering her voice and giving a friendly wave. She just couldn't help getting excited when she had a ter-ruff-ic idea!

"That's a good idea, Flash," Glitter said. "What kind of—"

Glitter stopped short. Flash had gotten to her paws and was now racing around the room, stopping every few feet to study the walls.

"Aha!" she barked, running back to join her friends and barking fast. "I knew I'd seen it somewhere. There's a map over there for Whisker Key, an island where Cutiecorn cats live. I'd bet my tail that's where the kittens came from!"

Sparkle laughed. "You figured that out before we could even shake a paw!"

"They don't call her Flash for nothing," Twinkle said with a smile.

"But how did they get here, to Puppypaw

Island?" Glitter wondered aloud. "And why do so many of their pranks involve us?"

Flash took another bite of muffin. Whisker Key was far, far away, so the only way for the kittens to reach Puppypaw Island was by boat. Did they have their own boat? Were they stowaways?

Stowaways! Flash clapped a paw over her mouth.

"I think I know how they got here," she said quietly. She had a sinking feeling in her stomach, like it was suddenly filled with globs of heavy peanut butter.

All three of Flash's friends turned to look at her quizzically.

"They must have come by boat, right? And

whose boat docked just before this kitten craziness began?" Flash said.

Sparkle gasped. "Your dad's!"

"Oh, Flash, you don't think the kittens stowed away on your dad's boat, do you?" Glitter asked.

Twinkle looked thoughtful. "It does make barking good sense. That could even be why the kittens have been playing so many tricks that affect you, Flash."

"We have to fix this!" Flash said, feeling her energy surge. "My dad could get in trouble for accidentally taking those little kittens so far from home. We need to get them back to Whisker Key, and fast!"

"But we don't have a boat," Sparkle said.

Flash grinned. "No, but we have a ferry. I'm sure we could ask old Captain Saltypaws to return the kittens to their home!"

"Puptastic thinking, Flash!" Glitter said. She glanced at the clock on the wall. "The ferry comes this afternoon. Bow wow, we don't have much time!"

Flash took one last slurp of her lemonade, brushed the muffin crumbs off her paws, and ran for the door. They had to get their tails in gear! She could hear her friends scrambling and laughing behind her as they tried to catch up.

"Where are you going, Flash?" Sparkle panted, bolting up alongside her.

"To the ferry dock!" Flash said. "That's where we need to lure the kittens, so that's where we should start."

The four friends ran along the twisty cobblestoned streets, past the town square (which was thankfully free of purple goo now), and down to the docks at the water's edge. Boats of all sizes were tied up there.

Flash finally skidded to a stop. Her friends plopped down next to her on the dock, huffing and puffing.

"Do you ever just walk anywhere, Flash?" Twinkle grumbled. "I could eat six more muffins after all that running."

Flash giggled. Grumpy Twinkle always made her laugh! Deep down, Twinkle was always ready to lend a paw, no matter how much she grumbled about it.

"Twinkle, I'll buy you a million muffins after we catch these kittens," Flash barked,

dancing around her friend. "But right now, we need you to use your seeing magic to figure out how to lure the kittens to the ferry dock. We have to get them on that ferry—before anyone figures out how they came here in the first place!"

They each had different magical specialties, and Twinkle's seeing magic was particularly strong. That meant she was good at solving complicated puzzles and riddles, and did a pawsitively wonderful job of understanding others, too.

Twinkle nodded and sat very still, her eyes closed in concentration. Before long, her ice-blue horn began to glow, faintly at first, then stronger and brighter. Suddenly, she jumped to her paws, a wide smile stretching across her snout.

"I've got it!" she cried. "What do kittens love more than anything?"

"Yarn!" Flash offered.

"Jingly bells!" Sparkle guessed.

"Fish!" Glitter added with an excited bark.

Twinkle nodded. "All those, and more. If we're going to catch these kittens, we have to use their favorite things. Even then, we'll need every ounce of magic we have between the four of us. These kittens are feisty—we can't let them get distracted along the way!"

Under Twinkle's direction, the four friends dashed around, gathering as much kitten bait as they could find. Soon, they all stood around a heaping pile of yarn, bells, cans of sardines, and dishes of milk.

"Sparkle and Glitter, you stay here at the dock and get ready for kitten chaos," Twinkle instructed. "Place some sardines along the dock, with a big bowl of milk right at the end. When we reach the ferry, talk to Captain Saltypaws and ask if he can take the kittens home to Whisker Key."

"Aye, aye!" Sparkle said with a salute. She paused for a minute, and her golden horn glowed. "My feeling magic tells me the kittens haven't gone far from where we last saw them. Head back toward the courtyard and keep your ears open for meowing mischief!"

"Got it. Flash, you're coming with me," Twinkle barked. "Grab as much as your paws can carry—we're going to find those kittens!"

Chapter 9

Loaded up with yarn and bells, Flash and Twinkle darted quickly back up to the courtyard where they'd last seen the kittens. But they were barking up the wrong tree—no such luck! Thanks to Sparkle, though, they knew that the kittens couldn't have gone far.

Just then, they heard a series of thumps and thuds around the corner. Without a bark, they followed the sound back out onto the street. It was coming from the Icy Paws Ice Cream Shop!

The sign out front said CLOSED, but the door was slightly open. So much noise was coming from inside, it sounded like there was a party going on!

Flash looked at Twinkle wryly. "Kittens," she said.

"Kittens," Twinkle agreed.

Sure enough, as they peeked in the front picture window, they could see the four kittens frolicking and pouncing around the shop! Worse, they'd figured out how to work the soft-ice-cream machines. There was ice cream everywhere! As they watched, the orange kitten grabbed a pawful from the machine and threw it at the calico kitten like a snowball.

Splat! The calico giggled as she licked ice cream from her whiskers.

"This is a doggone disaster," Flash said, watching with wide eyes. "We've got to get those crazy kittens out of Icy Paws!"

Twinkle nodded. "It's time to put our plan into action. Ready?"

"You bet your bark I'm ready!" Flash cried. She quickly attached the bells to her collar, and handed the ball of yarn to Twinkle. Then she hid right outside the door, pawfectly still, while Twinkle stepped into the shop.

"Oh, I'm sorry to interrupt!" Twinkle said to the kittens. "I just found this pawsome ball of yarn outside, and wondered if it belonged to one of you?"

The kittens meowed in surprise, prancing toward Twinkle in excitement. "How purrfectly kind of you!" the black-and-white one said.

Outside, Flash rolled her eyes.

"You can just paw it over," the gray one added.

There was a long pause, and Flash knew that Twinkle was using her seeing magic to figure out a plan to lure the kittens away. "Oh, I'm so glad the yarn made its way back to you," Twinkle barked after a moment. "Have you seen the way it glitters in the sunlight? It's really ter-ruff-ically sparkly—look!" With that, she opened the door and set paw outside, still holding the yarn. "Oops!"

Twinkle pretended to trip, dropping the ball of yarn. It rolled a few feet, but before it came to a stop, Flash focused all her attention on the yarn. She felt her horn begin to glow . . . and the yarn kept rolling!

It picked up speed as the kittens tumbled out of Icy Paws, their eyes flashing with delight. "After it!" the little orange kitten cried.

Flash dashed on ahead, keeping her eyes and her magic on the ball of yarn, rolling it down streets and around corners with ease. As she ran alongside it, the bells on her collar jingled merrily, letting the kittens know where the yarn was going so they didn't lose track of it. Behind her, Flash could hear the kittens leaping, pouncing, and racing along as fast as their little paws could take them. They mewed and giggled loudly. The chase was on!

As Flash came down the hill, closer to the docks, Twinkle ran out of a side street to join her. "Shortcut," she woofed. She glanced behind them. "One of the kittens is flying again."

Flash laughed. "Well, hopefully she'll fly right onto the ferry. Look!" Up ahead, they could see the ferry moored at the end of the longest dock. Sparkle and Glitter stood on either side of the dock, bouncing on their paws as they watched the kittens skitter down the hill.

Just then, the ball of yarn began to unravel.

As it rolled, the ball grew smaller and smaller. The kittens caught the end of it and pounced, tangling themselves up in the yarn as they tumbled head over paws in a big heap.

Flash and Twinkle skidded to a stop. What now? They hadn't made it to the dock yet, and the kittens were totally distracted—and tangled up, too!

Before they could think of what to do, Glitter bolted up the hill and approached the kittens. Her pink horn glowed, and Flash knew that her caring magic was in full effect. "Hi there," she said to the kittens in a friendly voice. "You look like you've got your fur in a twist. Can I help you out?" The kittens stopped wriggling and squirming, waiting patiently while Glitter untangled them from the yarn.

"Thanks," the black-and-white kitten mewed gratefully, smiling at Glitter.

"Anytime!" Glitter barked, her horn sparkling in the sunlight. "Hey, you must be thirsty after all that running around. Would you like some milk?"

All four pairs of kitten eyes lit up at the mention of milk. The calico cat got so excited she flew up into the air again! Licking their lips eagerly, they followed Glitter toward the docks.

Grateful for her friend's quick thinking and pawsome magical skills, Flash took the jingle bells off her collar and tucked them behind a potted plant. She didn't want to distract the kittens now! Quietly, she and Twinkle followed them to the bottom of the hill.

"Right this way!" Sparkle said, waving a paw to greet the kittens. "Sardines and milk for everyone!"

The kittens purred with excitement, stepping onto the dock and eagerly gobbling up the first of the sardines. They worked their way along the dock, racing from one tiny fish to the next. But suddenly, the gray kitten skidded to a stop. She looked from one side to the other in a panic.

"Uh-oh," Flash said under her breath as she and Twinkle joined Sparkle.

"I don't like water!" the gray kitten screeched nervously. Her friends all stopped, too, noticing the water surrounding them for the first time. "It was purrfectly scary when we accidentally tumbled onto that dog's boat as we were playing yesterday!"

This was it. They were going to turn around. The crazy kittens were so close to the ferry, and now they weren't going to set paw on the boat. If they stayed on Puppypaw Island, soon everyone would realize what mischief-makers they were. Flash's dad would surely be up to his snout in trouble for bringing them here!

Flash racked her brain. She had to do something! What else did kittens like that they hadn't tried yet?

Barking bulldogs—she had an idea!

Concentrating hard, Flash felt her horn begin to glow again. This time, she tried to focus all her energy, all her magic, into a little point of light. She'd never done this before! It took a moment, but soon she could see the point of light reflecting off a nearby pole. She tipped her head downward until the light appeared on the dock itself. Then, slowly, she moved it toward the kittens. Her horn was like a laser pointer!

The light bobbed up next to the scared gray kitten, and her head turned quickly to

look at it. She froze. She sat back on her haunches. Then—she pounced!

As she did, Flash moved the light farther down the dock. The kitten chased after it gleefully, forgetting all about the water on either side of her. As she leaped here and there, trying to catch the light, her friends noticed what she was doing . . . and as Flash had hoped, they wanted in on the fun!

Soon, all four kittens were bolting after the little point of light bobbing down the dock. They chased it closer and closer to the ferry, giggling and yowling, until Flash directed the light up the ferry ramp and right onto the boat. All four kittens jumped for it at once— and landed on the ferry in a pile!

No sooner had they set paw on the boat than it pulled away from the dock. Flash jumped into the air and let out a bark of triumph.

Flying fur balls—that was close!

Chapter 10

"Bye, little kittens!" Flash called. "Captain Saltypaws will get you home safely!"

On the upper deck of the ferry, the captain saluted her with a smile. He was an old gray Sheepdog, and had been driving the ferry for as long as anyone on Puppypaw Island could remember.

"Thanks for your help, Captain!" Sparkle

shouted, waving a paw. She turned to her friends. "He really shook a tail getting that boat away from the dock, didn't he?"

Glitter winked at Captain Saltypaws. "He sure did!"

On the lower deck, the four kittens waved their tiny paws back at their new puppy pals. They all had wide grins on their faces.

"I'm glad the kittens aren't mad at us for tricking them," Glitter said.

Twinkle snorted. "Are you kidding? They just got to do the most fun kitty obstacle course of all time! Who could be mad after that?" She flopped down on the dock and stuck out her tongue dramatically. "Though I could really use a nap right about now. All that running!"

Flash breathed a huge sigh of relief. The kittens were on their way home, and her dad hadn't gotten in trouble. Whew! She was ready for Puppypaw Island to get back to normal!

She looked out over the sparkling water. Boats dotted the horizon, and fluffy white clouds bobbed in the sky. What a truly ter-ruff-ic place to live! (Especially now that it wasn't covered with purple goo and mischie-vous kittens!)

"Who wants some food? I'm starving," she yipped, clapping her paws.

Twinkle grinned. "I think I know where we can find the perfect chilly treat . . . and lend a paw at the same time."

Flash's eyes sparkled. "Icy Paws!" she barked happily. "Oh, Sparkle and Glitter, you're not going to believe the mess those kit-tens made in there. Ice cream everywhere!"

"Then I guess it's a good thing you're hun-gry," Glitter said.

Flash dashed ahead, barking over her shoulder, "Last one there has to clean the Freezypaws machine!"

*　*　*

On Monday morning, Flash and her friends made their way to school just as they had the week before—but with no trip-ups or mysterious daisy chains this time! When they trotted through the big front doors of Cutiecorn Academy, Mrs. Horne was standing in the sunny entryway with a smile on her snout.

"Just the pups I was hoping to see!" she barked.

Flash looked at her friends. Oh grrrrrreat, were they in trouble?

"I heard you four had quite the adventure this weekend," Mrs. Horne said with a smile. Before any of them could bark, she added, "Yes, I know all about those silly kittens.

What a bunch of meowing mischief-makers!"

"H-how did you find out?" Sparkle stammered in surprise.

Mrs. Horne winked and whispered, "I have my ways."

Flash could hardly believe her ears! Mrs. Horne was even more magical than she'd thought.

"The most important thing is that the kittens are home safe with their families," Mrs. Horne said. "The four of you did a truly ter-ruff-ic job of tracking them down and sending them back home. You were quick on your paws, curious, kind, and thoughtful. Best of all, you were able to find and use your magic in all different situations—even when the stakes were high."

Mrs. Horne held out a paw, and four silver charms glimmered there. They were shaped like many-pointed stars. Flash couldn't help gasping at the sight of them. They were paw-somely beautiful!

"When I gave you your charm bracelets at the Enchanted Jubilee, I mentioned that you'd be able to earn additional charms," Mrs. Horne

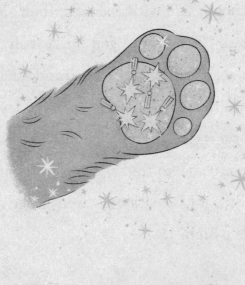

went on. "I think all of you have certainly earned this one! When you look at it, remember that the sparkle of magic is inside each one of you, and that you can access it anytime." She handed each pup a charm, then smiled and waved a paw. "I'll see you in class!"

Flash jumped up and down with excitement. In fact, she was bouncing so much that she could barely hold on to her new charm!

"Give me that!" Twinkle barked, laughing. "Now hold still. Don't you ever stop moving?" She carefully added the charm to Flash's shiny silver bracelet.

"Never!" Flash yipped, leaping into the air in excitement. She raced off down the hallway with her three best friends right on her tail. "See if you can keep up!"

About the Author

Shannon Penney doesn't have any magical powers, but she has ter-ruff-ic fun writing about them! If she were a Cutiecorn, she'd have a turquoise horn and the ability to turn everything to ice cream. For now, she'll settle for the ice and snow of New Hampshire, where she writes, edits, and goes on adventures with her husband, two kids, and two non-magical cats.

DON'T MISS THE CUTIECORNS' NEXT
ADVENTURE: RAINY DAY RESCUE.

Chapter 1

"I've got it!" Glitter barked, racing across the sand. She skidded to a sudden stop, stood up on her back paws, and bopped the colorful beach ball with her nose. It sailed over the volleyball net and landed just behind her friend Sparkle.

"Bow wow! What a shot!" A little ball of brown fur appeared at Glitter's side, panting and grinning. Flash was a Yorkshire Terrier with boundless energy—the pawfect volley-ball partner!

Sparkle and Twinkle ducked under the net to give Glitter high fives. "Not bad," Twinkle said with a shrug. The Beagle was known for being a little gruff and grumpy, but she was always there for her friends. She winked at Glitter and gave her a little smile.

"At this rate, Twinkle and I are going to lose this game in the twitch of a tail," Sparkle woofed with a giggle. The afternoon sunshine reflected off the golden horn on Sparkle's head. It glimmered so brightly that Glitter had to shield her eyes with a paw!

"You're going to blind someone with that thing!" Flash joked.

Glitter couldn't help but laugh. It was a beautiful day with not a cloud in the sky, and Sparkle's horn *was* awfully bright in the sunlight! All of the pups had horns between their ears, each in a different color—Twinkle's was blue, Flash's was purple, and Glitter's was a beautiful pearly pink. They weren't ordinary puppies. They were Cutiecorns! Their horns gave them pawsome powers, which made their home, Puppypaw Island, a truly magical place to live.

"It's our serve," Glitter said, carrying the beach ball across the sand.

As she waited for her friends to get into place, Glitter took a deep breath of the salty sea air. Gentle waves lapped at the sand on one side of her, and grassy dunes rose on the other. A light breeze ruffled Glitter's white fur. She peered around the mostly empty beach, thinking about how lucky they were to call Puppypaw Island home.

Just then, something in the tall beach grass near the volleyball net caught her eye. She stopped and squinted through the sunshine. Bow wow, it was a little French Bulldog! Glitter knew most of the pups on Puppypaw Island, but she had never seen this one before. He was mostly tan, so he blended into the sand, but he had a black muzzle and sweet black eyes. Two big ears stood tall on top of his head, with a royal-blue horn between them.

"Hi there!" Glitter called, waving a paw.

The pup looked around in alarm, clearly worried that he'd been spotted.

Glitter smiled and trotted over to him, leaving the beach ball behind. "I'm Glitter," she said with a friendly smile. "I'm sorry we didn't see you there sooner!"

The pup gave her a small smile in return. "I'm Batty," he said quietly. "I didn't mean to interrupt your game. It just looked like you were having so much fun! I had to stop and watch."

Glitter lowered her voice to a whisper. "We're having a pawsome time, but I think my friends Sparkle and Twinkle need some help. Would you like to play? They could really use you on their team!"

Batty blushed. "Really? I'm new here, and I've never played this game before."

"Well, this is a great way to learn!" Glitter said. "Where are you from?"

"My dad is a fisherpup, so we've traveled around a lot," Batty explained. "But now that I'm getting older, we're settling down in one spot. We just moved into a little house on the water." He pointed a paw off down the beach.

Glitter beamed. "It's furbulous to meet you. Welcome to Puppypaw Island!" She turned and waved her friends over. "Guys, this is Batty. I thought he could join Sparkle and Twinkle's team, since they're struggling against the Puptastic Duo!"

"Hey!" Sparkle protested, laughing. She looked at Twinkle and shrugged. "We could probably use the help."

"Bark for yourself," Twinkle said, giving Batty a sly wink. "But the more the merrier!"

Batty's face broke into a wide grin, and he

jumped to his paws. "Ter-ruff-ic!" he cried, darting across the sand in excitement.

The older pups followed, heading back to their places on either side of the net. "That was really nice of you, Glitter," Flash whispered, nudging her friend. "He looks so happy!"

Glitter felt cozy inside as she picked up the beach ball. Caring magic was her specialty, so helping others just came naturally to her. She loved how a small gesture could turn someone's day from just okay to pawsitively grrrrreat!